CLASS ACTS

MONOLOGUES FOR TEENAGERS

Class Acts: Monologues for Teenagers
First published 1998 by
New Island Books
2 Brookside
Dundrum Road
Dublin 14
Ireland

British Library Cataloguing in Publication Data
A catalogue record for this book is available from the British Library

ISBN 1 874597 78 2

New Island Books receives financial assistance from The Arts Council (An Chomhairle Ealaíon), Dublin, Ireland.

Cover photo: Enda O'Brien courtesy of Dublin Youth Theatre
Cover Design: Slick Fish Design, Dublin
Typesetting: New Island Books
Printed in the Republic of Ireland by Colour Books, Dublin

CLASS ACTS

MONOLOGUES FOR TEENAGERS

Clare Dowling and Caroline Williams

New Island Books

About the Authors:

Clare Dowling is an established playwright and screenwriter. Her plays include *Burn Both Ends, Leapfrogging* and *Small City*. She has also co-written children's books and an Internet serial for young people. At present she is writing for *Fair City*.

Caroline Williams is a theatre producer and editor. She devised and produced *There are no Irish Women Playwrights 1& 2*, and has researched for RTE/BBC. She has worked in the book trade as a drama buyer for several years.

Acknowledgements:

The authors wish to thank the following for their assistance with *Class Acts*: Fionnuala Abbot, Peter Williams, Iseult Sheehy, Vivienne Parry, Dermot Bolger, Ciara Considine and all at New Island Books.

CONTENTS

BOYS

Prologue

Welcome to *Class Acts*, our collection of original monologues for the classroom. Our aim with this collection is to produce monologues which are highly dramatic in their form, while capturing a young person's interest with topics that are both stimulating and relevant to their own lives.

A few pointers:

1. **FUN:** Though a lot of the issues covered may be of a serious nature, we hope that they are balanced by exuberant improvisations and drama games. It is perhaps easier to begin with some of the lighter pieces (e.g. Winner Takes All, Hasta La Vista Baby, Chips with Everything, etc.) A good discussion starter would be to ask members of the class to invent a history of the monologue character. Where do you think they live? What do they wear? What music do they like? etc.

2. **BALANCE:** In most cases we have made the points for discussion as general as possible. Where a discussion becomes very one-sided we would urge you to remember that some class members may hold the opposing view but are reluctant to say so.

3. **TACT:** Remember that in every class there may be students who have direct personal experience of the various issues. They have a right to privacy and the support of their teacher is vital.

Lastly, we hope that *Class Acts* will be both a useful and enjoyable tool for teaching and learning through drama.

Clare Dowling and Caroline Williams

Introduction

It is a grave mistake to consider young people as the theatre audience and participants of tomorrow. They are the theatre audience and participants of today — their involvement with theatre being just as valid and perhaps far more vivid (in the way that all experience is startlingly vivid when encountered for the first time) than that of their adult counterparts.

Too often however the scenarios and language with which they have to explore those first theatrical experiments don't fit properly — they belong to adult characters or to times and locations which are simply too far removed from their own everyday lives to resonate and become flesh and blood for them.

Therefore I can think of no other book in the canon of modern Irish drama which is quite like *Class Acts* in evoking, with breathtaking speed and authenticity, thirty moments of ordinary and yet extraordinary drama and tension drawn from the lives, fears and aspirations of contemporary teenagers.

Taken as a whole, this book exists like a box of masks for young actors and actresses to hide behind and to make real. It is a series of doorways into rooms and situations which are far wider than the brevity of each printed text suggests, as improvisations can grow and develop from each cameo, leading onto longer pieces of theatre to be scripted by the participants themselves.

Clare Dowling and Caroline Williams are to be saluted for burrowing so deeply and perceptively into the joys, anxieties and confusions of modern teenage life. Because in the end all theatre is about magic and creating the space to believe. These thirty sharp, short and punchy playlets do just that — inviting themselves to be interpreted in a thousand ways by as many young actors and actresses discovering and creating their own truth within each one.

Dermot Bolger

DEAR DA

NIAMH/CIARÁN AGE 13

Dear Da,

I hope you're well and I'm sorry for not writing last week as usual only Sandy went and had six puppies and two of them died and I was a bit upset and Ma got annoyed and said it was just as well because we could barely feed ourselves never mind six puppies and that's when I shouted at her and she told me to get upstairs until I found some manners and so I missed the five o'clock post and that's why you didn't get a letter from me. Anyway. Sorry. And I'm not complaining about Ma, we get on fine most of the time. And she didn't mean that bit about not having enough to eat either, honestly, so don't say anything to her about it. She'd kill me.

So. School is going well. I'm working very hard this term. I'm falling behind a bit in maths now that you're not here to help me in the evenings. Ma tries but she was always much better with geography. Maybe we can catch up at Christmas when you come to visit. I know it won't be like other Christmases but you'll stay for dinner at least, won't you? I already asked Ma if you could but she didn't say much. I think she misses you,

Da. She probably wouldn't tell you herself, so I thought I would.

The lawnmower broke down on me again yesterday. I think the rubber belt might be gone on it. Me and Ma had a look but we nearly chopped our fingers off so I think I'll wait until you visit and can fix it.

I wish you didn't have to move so far away, Da. I know that you had to leave, that you and Ma needed a break from each other and all that, I'm not complaining or anything. But the house seems very quiet now with just the two of us. Yesterday we didn't bother cooking dinner at all, we sent out for a pizza instead. I ordered a pepperoni with extra cheese, your favourite. It was nice but neither of us was very hungry. Sandy liked it though, she ate the whole lot.

I'd better go now, it's my turn to clean out the kennel. I wish you could see the puppies Da, they're gorgeous. They won't really be puppies any more by the time you see them, which is a shame. I'm trying to think of names for them so if you've any ideas will you let me know?

I miss you, Da. Ma warned me not to be putting pressure on you or anything and I'm not, honestly. I just don't think there's any harm in saying that I miss you.

Love (name)

Points for discussion:

1. What difficulties do you think a young person faces when their parents separate?
2. What emotions do you think they feel?
3. Currently in most cases of separation, the children remain with the mother. Why do you think this is?

Improvisations:

1. Niamh/Ciarán's dad drops by to mend the lawnmower. Run the scene.
2. Niamh/Ciarán's mum wants to give Sandy to her brother who owns a farm.

   Niamh/Ciarán is heartbroken and angry. She/He rings up her dad and wants to go and live with him, taking the dog. What happens?

☆☆☆☆☆☆

HOME ALONE

ORLA/EOGHAN, AGE 14

Put the flour, butter and eggs into a bowl, add the milk slowly, and beat until ready. I mean, what does that mean, "beat until ready"? If I knew when it was ready, then I wouldn't need a stupid cookbook, would I? Last week, it advised me to "add salt and pepper to taste". The question is, how much salt and pepper do you add to get any kind of a taste? A pinch? Two pinches? A shovelful? I'm going to phone up and complain to the people who write this stuff, I really am. And even if I manage to get it right, it's still not going to taste a bit like the way Mum's rhubarb flan tastes. Nobody can cook like my Mum.

Not that she does much of that any more. I don't mean to sound mean or small or resentful, but I'll bet *you* don't have to rush home from school on Mondays and Wednesdays in order to cook the dinner. Dad gets landed with the job on Tuesdays and Thursdays and Mum gets away scot-free with only Fridays. But usually, she's so tired from her new job that we end up eating some greasy take-away stuff.

"If you have a fan-assisted oven, reduce cooking time." I mean, here's more of it. Reduce by how much? 5 minutes? More? I was happy when she got the job, I really was. It's well-paid, in a big firm, and we were all really proud of her. And even though it's a real pain sometimes, we all chip in with the housework and cooking, with varying degrees of success.

"Fold into a tin." Fold. Why can't they just say "put". Put it into a tin, in plain English.

But it's a different story when you come home to a cold, dark, empty house and you know there's going to be nobody home for hours. You've had a miserable day and you're dying to moan about it only there's no one there to listen. By the time Mum gets home, it's too late and I'm the one who ends up listening to her.

She seems happier too, and I hate that, even though I know I shouldn't. But she's like a different person since she went back to work, as though us at home were never really enough.

Right. "Cook until done." Did you ever hear such rubbish? How will I know it's done unless they tell me? Sometimes she asks me if everything is okay and says that she's still there if I want to tell her anything. But I don't want to tell her that last bit, about her seeming happier. She might say that it was true.

Points for discussion:

1. How much responsibility should teenagers have for housework?

2. What are the pros and cons of having two working parents?

Improvisations:

1. It's dinnertime and your family are not very appreciative of your latest creation. Let them know how you feel.

2. Mime Game. One person mimes a household job . . . until the others guess it correctly.

✫✫✫✫✫✫

WORDS DON'T COME EASILY

JUDY/PHILIP, AGE 14

They all think I'm as thick as a plank in my school. I don't care. For as long as I can remember, everyone's thought I'm as thick as a plank because I was always last at everything. I was the last in pre-school to tell the difference between the letters n and z, the last in infants to know how to spell my own name, and the last to learn how to write. I did come first once, though. I was the first to have a note sent to my parents, telling them that I was falling behind. I was only five and a half. You could say that it's been pretty much downhill from there.

At least I used to have some company. Michelle Ryan, a girl in my class, was even thicker than me. The rest of them used to put bets on which of us would come last in the English tests at school. Eventually Mrs. Dunne took us both aside. She asked us what the problem was, and Michelle, the big baby, burst into tears and said that words and letters just didn't make any sense to her. They didn't make any sense to me either but there was no way I was letting on, because I knew what would happen. Sure enough, Mrs. Dunne murmured something about dyslexia and suggested that Michelle Ryan move into the special class at school. The dud class, in other words, which is what everybody else calls it.

And how about you, she says to me, are you finding reading and writing hard too? I could have told her the same as Michelle, that the words seem to jumble up and down with a life of their own. That I can learn a line fifty times over only to go back to it and have to learn it all over again. That I get so frustrated sometimes that I hurl my school books across the room. And that I hate being called thick when I know that I'm smarter than most of the people in my class, but that doesn't seem to count if you can't even write your own address. But there was no way in hell that I was going to be shoved into the dud class, with my mates sniggering and laughing behind my back — and they can be brutal when they get going. I'm fine, I said, looking her straight in the eye. I'm just thick.

I've been in my own class with my own mates for a year now. But I'm getting more and more behind in everything and my grades are the school joke. Sometimes it's hard to take, especially when I try so hard. Michelle Ryan passed an English test for the first time in her life last week. You'd want to hurry up, she said to me at break today. I'm not going anywhere, I said. I'm just thick.

Points for discussion:

1. Why do you think Judy/Philip is reluctant to look for help?

2. Dyslexia, which literally means Word Blindness, is a very common condition, yet often goes undetected for years. How can schools help students with learning difficulties?

3. What other difficulties do you think a dyslexic person would face in our society?

Improvisations:

1. The teacher insists that Judy/Philip write out a passage on the blackboard. Judy/Philip refuses, but will not say why. She/he is sent to the Principal's office and finally makes a cry for help. Run the scene.

2. Noel/Aoife is travelling to Cork for a match. He/she cannot make sense of the train timetable. Yet the people in the train station are not being helpful. Run the scene.

SWINGS AND ROUNDABOUTS

CATHY/DIARMUID, AGE 15

Come down from there, Christopher! There are other kids waiting their turn too, you know! What? I am not trying to keep my voice down, I'm just . . . oh look Christopher, would you just sit on the slide properly and come on down? I mean it. You come down this second or I'm going to come up and get you! Do you hear me?

That's my brother up there on that slide – Christopher. He turned seventeen last birthday. He's way too old to be up on playground slides you might think, but nobody here seems to mind. They all smile indulgently and let him go ahead of them. I just stand here mortified, horrified and terrified that a group of my friends are going to walk through this park any second and see me trying to cajole my six foot brother off a kids' slide.

Christopher! You cannot come down the slide standing, repeat, cannot! Sit down, please, Christopher! I'll buy you an ice cream later, how about that, eh? No I am not hissing again, shut up! Okay, yes I *am* hissing, that's because everybody's looking at you, can you not see that? Now you'd better come down, Christopher, because I'm going home. See? I'm walking away, Christopher! I'm walking away!

Now everybody's looking at *me*, in that superior, judgmental way that only people who've never lived with the Christophers of this world can. I know what they're thinking — how could anybody be so horrible to that poor boy? What did he do to deserve a sibling like me? Easy for them to think, when they don't have to live with the real Christopher, the Christopher who throws tantrums and punches, who drops his dinner on the floor just for fun, who tags after me when I go to town on Saturday afternoons with my friends, telling me in the loudest voice possible that he loves me.

Okay Christopher, you win! I'm not going to walk away, but only because if I arrive home without you, I won't be popular, you hear? If it was up to me, I'd leave you here! I'm just going to sit down on this bench here and ignore you, Christopher. You'll come down when you're good and ready, won't you?

The whole park is watching now, you'd think it was some kind of circus. But you get used to that. He's only an object of curiosity to them, a freak even. To me he's just my brother.

He's grinning down at me now, knowing just how far he can push me. I glare back up, pretending to be mad, even though I never can be for long. He grins wider and blows a soppy kiss. I give in and kiss him back.

Points for discussion:

1. What pressures does a child with special needs place on a family and what impact do you think this has on siblings? What positive influences do you think Christopher has on his family?

2. What way do you think society treats people with special needs?

Improvisations:

1. Run the monologue situation using Cathy/ Diarmuid, Christopher, and other adults and children at the playground.

2. Christopher is being picked on by a bunch of younger children. Cathy/Diarmuid arrives on the scene.

3. Cathy/Diarmuid behaves like an older brother or sister towards Christopher. Run some improvisations of family life when they were much younger: 5 and 7; 9 and 11; 13 and 15 etc.

✵ ✵ ✵ ✵ ✵ ✵

JESUS SAVES

LAURA/ALAN, AGED 16

It makes me really angry the way people poke fun at it. My group leader says it's just ignorance and she's right. For starters, we don't go around saying stupid things like "I've found Jesus". Even though we have — found Jesus, I mean. But we don't push it down other people's throats and we keep ourselves to ourselves. We don't do anybody any harm, and we might even do a bit of good if only people would listen.

I joined up first because somebody listened. It was two years ago, when I was bogged down in all that meaning of life stuff, couldn't see beyond exams and pressure and there didn't seem to be any point to it all, at least for me. I tried to talk to my parents. Cheer up, said Mum. Here's twenty quid, said Dad. Then I met Susan. She's my group leader and she just walked right up to me in the park one day and said that I looked as if I needed to talk. And for the first time in my life, someone listened to what I had to say, I mean really listened. Mum says that it's typical, that these kind of people always hit on kids when they're at their lowest. But I just point out that Susan was there for me when my parents weren't. She has no answer to that.

It was strange at first. Susan invited me along to one of their youth evenings and I suppose I expected everyone to be playing guitars and eating tofu. But they were just ordinary people, people like me. That evening, we sat around and talked and played music and it was nothing at all to do with religion. I was able to tell Dad that there was no brain-washing or money-racketeering or free love going on. I think he was a bit disappointed.

I wasn't. In two years, my life has totally changed. I know who I am now and where I'm going. I work hard at school but I'm not obsessed with exams. I don't smoke or drink or sleep with people and that's my choice, not anybody else's. All in all, I think I turned out pretty okay, wouldn't you?

But I still get annoyed when people make fun of it. It's worse in school, where I know I'm an easy target. But I ignore them all. People who don't believe in Jesus are not the kind of people I want to be friendly with anyhow. And I get annoyed sometimes too with my parents, when they go on about cults and stuff. But mostly they make me sad when they tell me earnestly that this is just a teenage phase and that I'll grow out of it. I can't seem to get through to them that this is for life.

They don't believe in any God themselves. And that to me is the saddest thing of all.

☆☆☆☆☆☆

Points for discussion:

1. What way does religion provide "meaning" to life?

2. "People who don't believe in Jesus are not the kind of people I want to be friendly with . . . " Discuss this attitude.

Improvisations:

1. Set up a stand to convince passers-by to join your religion.

2. Laura/Alan's parents burst into one of the youth evenings and insist that she/he leave with them. Run the scene.

☆ ☆ ☆ ☆ ☆ ☆

HOME AND AWAY

MICHELLE/LIAM, AGE 16

Honey, is that you home? she calls from the top of the stairs. Her voice is this horrible high-pitched squeal which lapses into an American accent from time to time even though she was born and bred in Drimnagh. Honey? Would you ever pop down the shops for some milk? Now, here is a woman who doesn't work, who doesn't have kids of her own, whose only commitment in the entire day is an episode of Home and Away, and she still can't find time to buy a pint of milk. Dad says she's sick today but I know it's only an excuse. Sorry, I shout through gritted teeth, but I'm doing my homework! Silence for a moment, then here she comes, clunk-clunking down the stairs in fluffy pink slippers and a bathrobe that's at least a size too small. She cocks her head to one side and smiles, all sticky red lipstick even in the middle of the day. How was school? she asks, as though she really cares. Fine, I snap, turning a page, dismissing her. You can tell she'd rather be anywhere but here. I like seeing her uneasy — she often is when Dad's not home. You should see the way she runs to him at the door, as if she's been saved. And the way he looks at me, as if accusing me of upsetting her in his absence. Like I'd be bothered.

It's as hard on her as it is on us, he said to me one night, try to see that. I got very angry then. All I see, I said, is a cheap woman with an eye on the main chance who moved in before Mum was even cold in her grave. He slapped me then. I slapped him right back. It's good to clear the air, isn't it?

Can I help at all? she asks now, leaning over my homework. I seriously doubt it, I say, not bothering to look her in the face. She gives up then, and searches in a pocket for a pound coin. Just a pint if you wouldn't mind, she mumbles, before clunk-clunking back up the stairs. And then I see it, a flash of pink, her night-gown hanging down. It's one of Mum's. That woman is wearing one of my Mum's night-gowns. I pick up the pound coin and flick it hard. It flies through the air and hits her square in the back. She stands in frozen shock for a moment. Then she picks up the money and goes on upstairs, back stiff with anger and pride. Suddenly I feel like crying. I go back to my homework instead.

Points for discussion:

1. "It's as hard on her . . . " Is it?
2. Should children have a say in whether or not their parent's new partner moves in?

Improvisations:

1. Michelle/Liam brings home three friends. The new partner, Sheila, has just made muffins and chats to them — they think she's great . . . What happens now?

2. Michelle/Liam runs away to her/his granny's house in Cork. Sheila has to go and pick her/him up. Run the scene in the car using four people — two play the parts and have very stilted conversation, two do voice-overs of what's going on in their heads, what they're not daring to say to each other.

STREET LIFE

FIONA/BARRY, AGE 16

Fifteen ... fifteen fifty ... fifteen sixty ... seventy ... ninety ... ninety two ... three ... five. Fifteen pounds ninety five pence. Not bad, considering. It's been below freezing today, so not many people were out. But on a good day, you can make maybe twenty five quid, sometimes even thirty. Means you can stay in a hostel for the night and buy something hot to eat and still have a few quid left over. You'd give that to one of the others, Damien or Nikki, if they've had a slow day. They'd do the same for you, that's the way it is out here. I hate the way people think that we all live like a bunch of filthy sewer rats, robbing and thieving and stabbing each other in the back. I wash myself every day in one of the fast-food restaurants and I've never spent a penny that I didn't earn first. And nobody at home has ever looked out for me the way Damien and Nikki do out here.

God, it's cold today. Got to keep moving, keep the circulation going. One of the others, I didn't know him that well, he slept rough behind a clothing factory last month without even a blanket to cover him and he never woke up. It was all over the newspapers for days and we were hounded by trendy reporters slumming it to get a good story about "life on the streets". A week later we were forgotten again. The dead bloke's parents came down here and said it was our fault for encouraging him to stay away from home. We didn't even know why he'd left. It's not that we didn't care, it's just that everybody's got a story to tell. You just don't tell it.

Lucy will be along soon. She's this really nice woman from the social, she never misses a week. Mostly she just makes sure I'm all right, but sometimes she starts on about how I should go back home, how I should make it up with my family and think about school and the future. I just answer that I'm sixteen now and nobody can make me do anything that I don't want to. I know my rights. I think she's mostly worried that I'll get in with Louise Smith and that crowd, be out of my head all day and pulling down on the quays at night. But I'm not that stupid.

Sometimes I miss home, my Mum mostly. But it was her that drove me out in the end, when she wouldn't believe me. I suppose I should have known that she'd never choose me over him. Anyway, I left. I rang her once just to let her know that I was doing much better without her. I told her I was doing just fine. And I am.

☆☆☆☆☆☆

Points for discussion:

1. What do you think are the dangers young people face when they live on the street?
2. What would be a good way to protect young people who end up sleeping rough?

Improvisations:

1. In the character of Fiona/Barry do a television interview for a documentary on the homeless. You suspect the television crew are just exploiting your situation.
2. You're a runaway spending your first night sleeping on the street. What and who do you encounter?

☆ ☆ ☆ ☆ ☆ ☆

CHIPS WITH EVERYTHING

DEIRDRE/STEPHEN, AGE 17

Excuse me? Can you move your feet please, I'm trying to sweep the floor, thank you. Excuse me, sir ... thank you ... excuse me? ... thank you ...

It's only since I've started working here that I've seen what pigs people really are. They think nothing of chucking burger wrappings or spare straws or cigarette butts onto the floor for someone else to pick up. Yesterday, this bloke took the pickle from his burger, mayo and ketchup dripping off it, and he just tossed it over his shoulder, casual as you like. And as for the bathrooms ... I won't go into it, I can see you're trying to eat your double bacon wham o'burger, but the point I'm making is that customers are pigs for the most part. Excuse me, would you ever move your feet?

The staff aren't much better. They're mostly part-timers, college-kids who're only here to finance their social lives, smart-mouths who look down on us that work here full-time. How do you live on the wages they pay us, says this one to me last week in a superior voice. I live because I have to, I snapped back. Look, I don't mean to keep on at you, but would you ever move your feet? And you! Don't throw that on the floor!

A crowd from my old class came in today and sat just over there in their school uniforms. They ordered burgers and chocolate shakes and swapped stories about the mock English exam. I tried to hide out the back but the manager sent me out. You should have seen them all trying not to stare at my wham o'burger uniform, with the matching clogs. You should have seen the half-pitying, half-mortified looks on their faces. They didn't stay long and I know we won't meet up next week like we said we would. You — yeh, you over there! I'm not warning you again about throwing stuff on the floor! I'll get the doorman on you, I mean it!

I'm not normally in such a foul humour, it's just that today has been rough. Days like this kind of depress me. I thought it'd be different, you know? Thought that everything was there just for the taking. I said that school was a waste of time and that I had to get out there or the world would pass me by. Imagine. At fifteen!

Mum says I can always go back, and maybe onto college to get some qualifications. But I don't want to sit in a classroom with my kid sister and her mates, like some kind of geriatric. Naw. I'll muddle along here, it's not too bad for all the giving out I do, and the boss says that I might make assistant manager next year. Listen, I'm going on my break now, would you ever keep an eye on my brush?

Points for discussion:

1. Do you think Deirdre/Stephen was right to leave school so early?

2. Why do you think she/he won't meet up with her/his old school friends?

Improvisations:

1. Be a busy Fast Food Restaurant. Some hassled staff, some bossy managers, and some difficult customers. See how hectic you can make it . . . and how many rows you can avoid because the customer is always right!

2. Waiters and waitresses often have to endure a lot of bad manners from their customers. Try serving a table of particularly obnoxious customers — only this time, when they've provoked you enough, let them know just how difficult it is to do your job!

✿ ✿ ✿ ✿ ✿ ✿

JOB SEARCH

ANGELA/GARRET, AGE 17

The interview was worse than the toughest exam any teacher could throw at me. I sat in a tiny room with seventeen other hopefuls for the position of part-time supermarket shelf-stacker and grocery packer. There were only three jobs going and I knew it was going to be dog eat dog.

The first question on the application form I was handed completely stumped me. Why do you want this job, it asked. The money, I wanted to shout, but knew that this would probably not impress the manager. But it *was* the money, mostly — a bit of independence for once in my life, to be able to pay my own way. Instead I scrawled that I would welcome the opportunity to take on responsibility and be part of a team blah blah. It looked really pretentious the minute I'd written it but I was sure everyone else in the room had written the same thing.

Question number two was another brain teaser. What can you offer this company? My head started to ache. A decent sense of humour probably didn't count. How about the ability to tolerate obnoxious customers? Found myself putting down words like team spirit, punctuality and reliability. The swotty looking guy beside me asked for another page.

Question number three wasn't any better — could I please list my weaknesses.

Oh God. Chocolate was the obvious answer but I knew they were looking for major personality defects. I was tempted to put down none. I ended up waffling on about my inability sometimes to make decisions and my impatience with red tape. By the time I was finished I had put myself across as paranoid, intolerant and with possible psychopathic tendencies.

I was the first in the room to finish the questionnaire. Everyone around me was asking for extra pages, heads bent industriously. I looked over my application form one final time and decided it was rubbish. I crossed it all out and wrote down what I really thought in two minutes flat. I said that I really wanted the job because I needed the spare cash, I thought it might be a bit of fun and that I was, on the whole, a reliable and honest human being. Then I got up and left.

The phone call came the next day. Was I free on Saturdays and on school holidays? Certainly, I said very solemnly, and thanked the manager. I put down the phone and jumped around the room. Yes yes yes! I had the job! I had just joined the ranks of the employed.

✵ ✵ ✵ ✵ ✵ ✵

Points for discussion:

1. What are the pros and cons of having a part-time job while you're in school?
2. What do you think are good jobs and what do you think are bad jobs for young people to do?

Improvisations:

1. It's Angela/Garret's first Saturday in the supermarket. Run the scene.
2. Angela/Garret tells her/his parents with great delight about their new job. Her/His parents say no way are they allowed to work until the exams are over. Run the scene.
3. Anna/John works in a restaurant three nights a week until 1 A.M. It is her/his Leaving Cert year and she/he hasn't told the school about her job. Her/his Irish teacher arrives for a meal with his family. What happens?

☆☆☆☆☆☆

GIRLS'
Monologues

RED HANDED

NICOLA, AGE 13

Hello? Hello, is anybody out there? Could I get a glass of water please? Can anybody hear me? Hello . . . ?

I think they're ignoring me on purpose. I wish they'd let Jennifer stay with me, at least it'd be company, but they hauled her off to another cell. They said that they were going to call our parents before they decided what to do with us. Oh God. I'm really going to be murdered this time.

I wouldn't mind, but it was a horrible blouse. Red satin, I wouldn't wear it in a fit. I don't know what possessed me to steal it, I really don't. I've never so much as dodged a bus fare in my life, and there I go robbing a vile blouse for some stupid dare. Jennifer said that it'd be a breeze, that she'd watch for in-store cameras while I slipped it in my bag. We didn't get two steps out the door before I felt a hand descend on my shoulder, every shopper's nightmare. The security guard very politely asked us would we accompany him back inside. Jennifer said in her haughtiest voice that she hoped he wasn't accusing us of actually stealing anything. He pointed then, and I looked down to see the sleeve of the red blouse trailing along the ground from my bag. As they say in the business, we were nicked.

In the manager's office, Jennifer turned on the tears straightaway. The manager wasn't a bit impressed. He gave her a hanky and called the guards. For our own good, he said. Everyone watched as two uniformed police marched us through the store and into a waiting squad car. I've never been so embarrassed in all my life. Just as we were being driven away, I saw the astonished face of my Mum's best friend.

Oh no. What are my parents going to say? Dad's nose will swell and go red the way it does when he's really furious. And Mum's lips will go pinched, the way they do when she's very upset about something. They're the kind who always blame themselves, you know what I mean? All over a stupid red satin blouse.

One the guards said to me earlier that I'm the lucky one. I didn't know what he meant. He told me that Jennifer already had two cautions for shoplifting and that the store would probably prosecute. He said that they wouldn't be pressing charges against me, because I came from a decent family. In his softest voice, he told me it might be a good idea if I didn't steal anything ever again. I kind of agreed with him.

Hello? Hello, can anybody hear me? Hello? Is there anybody out there at all?

Points for discussion:

1. Should Nicola be punished? How?

2. Some shopping centres ban school uniform wearers. Is this a sensible policy?

3. Your best friend gives you a very expensive birthday present. You strongly suspect she stole it. What do you do?

Improvisations:

1. Ask two class members to be Nicola's parents. They've just got the telephone call from the Gardai. What way would they react?

2. Nicola returns to school. Her whole class knows what happened. Be that class — some teasing, some condemning, some supporting.

3. Mime: You're in a department store. You haven't stolen anything, indeed you have no intention of stealing anything. Yet the security guard has been watching and making you nervous . . . so you begin to act suspiciously, because you're so uncomfortable being watched. The security guard is alerting all the staff that you are up to something and you begin to take offence!

✵ ✵ ✵ ✵ ✵ ✵

A CRUSHING DEFEAT

GRAINNE, AGE 14

Mum says I'm a hopeless romantic, but I never meant to go falling in love that Monday morning, honest. I was busy dissecting a frog with Miriam Wallace, my science partner, when I looked up and there he was — all clean and crisp in a new white lab coat, his dark hair falling in sensuous waves over his forehead. He had these moody brown eyes, hard and uncompromising, and a mouth that you'd just die for. When he spoke, his voice was gravelly and low and sent shivers down my spine. Even his name was like something straight out of a film. Mark Jackson, he said he was, our substitute science teacher while Mrs. Brennan was off having her twins. He smiled then, a kind of sulky, bored smile, and half the girls in the class nearly collapsed. The other half *did* collapse when my frog, not quite dead, made a wild bid for freedom across the lab. In the midst of the mayhem, Mark Jackson's eyes met mine and that's when it happened. It wasn't my fault. Nobody can help falling in love, can they?

Mum says I can be a bit obsessive sometimes, but I never meant for things to go this far, honest. I just wanted to let him know how I felt, that was all, in case maybe he felt the same way too. So I started giving him burning looks over the test-tubes and writing cryptic little notes on my assignments. Soon I was hanging around the staff room at break, smiling at him as he went in and out. I stuck cuddly toys under his windscreen wipers and once I pretended to faint at his feet in class. I even sent him a Valentine's card, with my name on it, plain as day. I got a bit annoyed after a while when he didn't give any indication that he noticed how much I cared. And maybe things got a bit out of hand then, but I never meant to do any harm.

Mum says that she's found a new school now, way out in the suburbs, where I start next week. It's an all-girls school, run by the nuns. She says that I can start fresh there, where nobody knows about Mark Jackson or the anonymous telephone calls or the hours I spent watching his house. She promised that she hadn't told anybody about the complaints he made to the headmistress and that awful day he shouted at me to leave him alone. I didn't so much mind that as the fact that he couldn't remember my name. You know the way you can always tell when someone's forgotten your name? I looked hard at him then, a thin man with small, beady eyes and a mean mouth and I told him that I was very sorry. And I am. I never meant to do any harm. Honest.

❊ ❊ ❊ ❊ ❊ ❊

Points for discussion:

1. What is a crush?

2. "Nobody can help falling in love ..." Is this true?

Improvisations:

1. Grainne's best friends try to take her mind off Mr. Jackson. Run the scene.

2. Grainne gets into Mr. Jackson's car and refuses to get out until he declares his love for her. Involve passers by, her friends, his colleagues, the principal etc. if appropriate!

3. Mr. Jackson goes into the staff room, rumours are flying among his colleagues, what happens?

✻✻✻✻✻✻

LATE ARRIVAL

REGINA, AGE 14

I'm embarrassed. No, I'm not just embarrassed, I'm absolutely, totally, completely mortified. I mean, how could she do this to me? My own mother? Getting pregnant again at the age of forty-one? Oh God, I think I'm going to die.

I mean, for starters, it was a terrible shock to know that your parents are still . . . you know. You'd think they'd be past all that stuff, you'd think they'd have more sense. And she's already showing, she's like a walking advertisement that she had my Dad have been . . . you know. They're holding hands all the time now, even at the kitchen table, her all coy and smiley and him so chuffed you'd swear he'd just climbed Everest with no oxygen. Ugh. I can't bear it, every time I look at the two of them I think of them . . . you know. They're my stuffy old parents, for God's sake, it just doesn't seem natural, does it?

And all my friends will know too. I'm going to get a terrible slagging. I tried to tell my Mum as tactfully as possible that she wasn't to show up at school any more with my forgotten lunches. But she missed the point entirely and got all girly with me. It'll be fun, she said, we can go shopping for maternity wear, you must know all the trendy shops. Can you imagine your hugely pregnant mother following you and your mates around Top Shop on a Saturday afternoon? I would die.

She thought in the beginning that we'd have some kind of a special relationship now, females together and all that. She kept showing me scans of a small squirmy creature that didn't look anything like a baby. She wanted me to put my hand on her stomach all the time, and to read up on the stack of pregnancy books she'd bought. I don't want to know, Ma, alright? I told her the day she started going on about her waters breaking and the rest. You go ahead and have your baby, I said, but it's nothing to do with me.

I'm angry too, I can't help it. I just think she's being really selfish. She's so wrapped up in the baby that she doesn't seem to notice me any more. It's like I'm a second class citizen now and have to move over to make room for a brother or sister that I don't want or need. We used to talk about things to do with me once in a while. Now she's either too tired or not interested.

Thank God I have you, she said yesterday and I felt a bit better. At least you'll be there to help out with it, she said, to baby sit once in a while. I got really annoyed then. I'm doing my Exams next year, I said, have you totally forgotten? She blinked at me then and I knew she had.

Regina will come around when it's born, I heard my Dad say to her this morning. Yeah, well, we'll see.

❄❄❄❄❄❄

Points for discussion:

1. Do you think Regina will come around?

2. What are the positive aspects of her situation?

3. How much responsibility do you think older brothers and sisters should have for their younger siblings?

Improvisations:

1. Breakfast, one week after the baby has been born. Baby has had a sleepless night . . . so has the rest of the household. Regina's mum asks her to give a hand. Run the scene.

2. Mime Game: Pass an imaginary baby carefully around, instructing as you pass — Rock to sleep, Feed, Play, etc.

❄❄❄❄❄❄

I WANT TO HOLD YOUR HAND

LORRAINE, AGE 15

Maybe I should just ask him straight out, no messing, and then I might find out where I stand. Just straight out, "Gary, are you ashamed of me?" And he'll whinge "No Lorraine, course I'm not ashamed of you, what put that into your head?" And I'll come right back with "Why d'you treat me like that in front of your mates then?" At which point he'll throw his eyes to heaven, sigh heavily and spread his hands helplessly, "Ah Lorraine, don't start that again, about me kissing you in front of me mates." And I'll say it's nothing to do with kissing — which it isn't — and he'll mumble that he hasn't the foggiest what I mean, but this time I'm not gonna let him off the hook, no way. Not after last night, when we were walking down the street and we were holding hands and standing real close and it was lovely, it really was — at least, until his mate Decko showed up and he dropped my hand like a hot potato and literally jumped away from me and went on ahead like he was ashamed to be seen with me! Like he didn't even know me! And us going out together nearly four months!

I'm gonna say it to him this time, I am. I'm gonna say, "Gary, I'm not asking you to be all over me like a rash. I'd just appreciate it if you didn't act so embarrassed that I'm your girlfriend, as if you couldn't pull anything better." If he likes me, and I know he does, then why is it such a big deal?

But I know what he'll say. "Ah come on Lorraine, will you ever stop reading so much into everything. We have a good time on our own, don't we, and that's all that matters. And anyway, you don't see other blokes all over their girlfriends, do you?"

And I'll get annoyed and say something about him just trying to be cool and then he'll get annoyed and say something stupid about hormones and that'll be that. End of conversation. You know, sometimes I think that men and women are just wasting their time with each other. They'll never get on.

Points for discussion:

1. Why is Gary embarrassed?

2. Why is Lorraine not embarrassed?

Improvisations:

1. Gary is teased by his mates, and sticks up for himself. Run the scene.

2. Gary and Lorraine are queuing for the cinema, suddenly they recognise some of their mates . . . What happens?

3. Run the improvisation above using <u>mime</u> only.

✷✷✷✷✷✷

THAT PLASTIC, IT'S FANTASTIC

ANNE MARIE, AGE 15

Fiona Johnson had it done. She was in desperate pain for weeks and weeks afterwards, but she had it done. Her lips. She said that they were non-existent and that she'd never get fella. If you ask me, the main stumbling block there is her personality, but there's no talking to some people. So she had them done. Her lips. Got some plastic stuff injected into them. They said the whole thing was a massive success, but between you and me, it looks like someone gave her a punch in the gob. And she still hasn't got a fella.

And now there's Bernie Moran on about her breasts. She reads loads of glossy magazines and she says that it's the height of fashion and that she's gonna get hers done for her birthday. Someone asked her whether she was getting them made bigger or smaller and she wasn't a bit impressed. Anyway, her Da only shares a milk round so it's hard to see where he'd get the kind of money it'd take to get his Bernie a boob job. I think she's mad.

My nose is fairly bad. No, seriously, it is, stop being nice. It's from my Ma's side, I've seen a photo of her grandmother in profile and it's easy to see where it all went wrong. Sometimes I get slagged about it, but I read glossy magazines too and I know all about shading and toning and on a good night, you wouldn't even notice it. Bernie Moran said that I should think about getting a nose job. I said that I would, but I won't really. I'd feel kind of funny with a nose that wasn't mine. Anyway, nobody's perfect, are they?

Points for discussion:

1. Why do people want to look "perfect"?

2. Is there more pressure on women than men?

3. Do media images of women/men contribute to this?

Improvisations:

1. Be a door-to-door sales person for plastic surgery. Keep this one moving, with a queue of sales people all making pitches!

2. Game: Sit in a circle and play I like my Nose with an N because it is . . . (Nice, Notorious, Neat etc.) People can choose any body part they like but the letter must match i.e. I Like my Eyes with an E because they are . . . (Enchanting, Exotic etc.) Keep going around the circle as long as you can. Adjectives can be as ridiculous as you like!

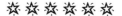

HASTA LA VISTA, BABY

SUSAN, AGE 15

Hello? Eh, por favor signor, I'm holding for Carlos . . . he works in the hotel bar . . . Hello, Carlos, is that you? Oh Carlos, I can't believe I'm finally talking to you! What? It's Susan, Carlos! God, anybody would think you'd forgotten me already! Oh Carlos, these last two weeks have been desperate, I've spent days and days imagining this phone call and what we'd say to each other . . . You sound a bit funny Carlos, is everything alright? Anyway, I didn't ring before because you know what my parents are like. They still think it's a silly holiday romance and that we'll forget all about each other now that I'm home and you're still in Spain. Imagine! Carlos? Are you still there? Oh, right, must be just a bad line.

I showed the holiday snaps to all my mates and they said you were gorgeous, what do you think of that? And they were sick with jealousy when I said I might be going back to see you on my own at Easter! That's if Mum and Dad let me, of course. Did you talk to your parents about me staying in the house yet? Oh. I see. Well, I suppose you're right. Easter's a long time away and there's no point in rushing things yet.

So. Did you get my letters, Carlos? Yes, all sixteen of them, I did say I'd write every day. I've only got a postcard from you yet. Are the letters on the way? Oh. You've been too busy to write. Even one single letter, Carlos? There's no need to get snappy, I'm just asking, that's all.

So. Have you any more news for me? You're busy? Sorry, I didn't mean to keep you, I thought that the afternoons were usually quiet, but I guess my memory is playing tricks on me, eh? I won't take up any more of your time, so.

No, no, please don't promise to write or phone, Carlos, especially when we both know that you won't. And I was only joking, by the way, about coming over at Easter. I wasn't really serious, you know that, don't you? Listen, I have to go now, I've things to do, important things. Yeh. Yeh, maybe I'll see you next summer. Ce sera sera, you creep!

Points for discussion:

1. Do you think Carlos cared about Susan at all?

2. Are holiday romances always over on the last day of the holidays?

Improvisations:

1. Susan writes Carlos just one more letter beginning:

   Dear Carlos, you creep . . .

   Dictate the rest!

2. Pierre and Shona had a holiday romance in France. Shona came back, told a few of her friends, wrote once, maybe twice, then forgot all about him. On Christmas Day Pierre arrives on her doorstep to declare his undying love for her in his few words of English. Run the scene!

A LASTING PHASE?

PAULA, AGE 16

See her? That blonde girl over there? The one who's looking this way now? That's Emily Byrne. She once had a massive crush on Helen Leahy. Imagine! A girl liking a girl! Helen Leahy was years older than us and captain of the hockey team. She had brown hair and brown eyes and was nice looking if you like that kind of thing. Emily obviously did because it was love at first sight. We used to slag the life out of her — I mean, a girl liking a girl! She tried to hide it, but she'd go scarlet every time Helen's name was mentioned. That winter, she suddenly developed a huge interest in hockey and spent every evening panting after Helen around the outdoor pitch. But the best of all, she went and dyed her lovely blonde hair brown, just like Helen's. The very next week, didn't Helen go and dye hers blonde. God, we laughed. A girl liking a girl . . . I mean, we could understand girls getting crushes on the teachers, like that Maths teacher we had two years ago, he was all right. But another girl? We all thought Emily Byrne was mad.

But one by one, didn't Laura and Jennifer and Anne all get crushes on the older girls. You couldn't turn around only one of them would be blushing, or sending soppy Valentine cards, or dying their hair black or red or brown. There were so many of them in love with girls that it nearly became the norm. Nobody said they were disgusting or perverted or just plain stupid. And a year later, when they'd all gone off girls and were mad into guys, none of them was even embarrassed. It's just a phase, they'd tell the younger ones coming up, and everybody would laugh. It's just a phase and it'll pass.

Funny, isn't it. Now you'd be taking your life into your hands to admit that you liked another girl. They wouldn't laugh now, they wouldn't slag you in the classroom. They'd scrawl filth about you on the toilet doors and chase you home.

I'm too old now to go dying my hair blonde like Emily's, or to rush off and join the drama club just because she's playing the lead. I don't send her Valentines and I manage to control my blushes. I just pretend to be like everybody else and hope and pray that it's just a phase that will pass.

Points for discussion:

1. Do you think that Paula is a lesbian?

2. What difficulties do you think gay and lesbian people face in our society?

3. Why do you think that some heterosexual people react so negatively towards a gay or lesbian person?

Improvisations:

1. Paula is on a bus. Emily gets on and sits two seats in front. Run the scene using two people miming and two doing voice-overs for what's going on in their heads.

2. You suspect your best friend is gay but they haven't told you, so you offer them some encouragement. Run the scene.

3. It's Christmas Dinner — you've picked a very dramatic moment to come out as a gay or lesbian to your family. Run the scene.

✿✿✿✿✿✿

I MAKE ME SICK

ELIZABETH, AGE 16

1st April.

Lost two pounds, great. Daily intake: two fingers of Kit Kat, three oranges and a slice of bread. Ate a full dinner but puked it up again. Mum caught me coming out of the bathroom but I told her that I had a stomach upset. Fooled her completely. Total Calories 360, sit-ups 50. Very good!

2nd May.

Oh no. Terrible day. Went on a binge after everybody had gone to bed. Ate whole sliced pan with pot of jam, three bags of popcorn, a plate of cold, greasy ham and a block of ice cream. Lay in bed telling myself what a disgusting fat pig I was and hating myself. Total Calories about 25,000. Sit-ups none. A write-off. Will not eat another thing ever again. Must remember to replace the food in the kitchen.

17th June.

Almost fainted during gym class at school, but one look at skinny Liz Doyle made me determined to stick to diet this time. Mum was puzzled over four missing packets of biscuits that I forgot to replace.

Went to bed starving but happy because I weigh a pound less than I did this morning. Total Calories 10, sit-ups 100. Brilliant!

25th June.

Am still the same weight I was this time last month. Am so depressed I feel like topping myself. Spent an hour looking through glossy magazines of thin supermodels. If I looked like that I know I'd be happy. Went to bed early to take my mind off food. Total calories 560, sit-ups 25. Okay, but must do better tomorrow.

9th July.

Summer holidays are hell. Mum's watching me like a hawk all day. Was sick twice. Looked at my teeth in the mirror, they're gone all discoloured. Don't want to go out of the house to see all those skinny girls walking around in summer skirts and crop tops. Sit in my room thinking about how my life is going to change when I'm thin. Total calories 5,000, sit-ups 10. Really bad.

11th July.

Weighed myself sixteen times today, managed to put on two pounds in the space of an hour. How can that be? Made myself sick and cried myself to sleep. I have no will power or determination at all, I deserve to be fat.

16ᵗʰ July.

Terrible day. Mum caught me puking in the bathroom. Marched me down to doctor, who said that my weight was perfectly normal and that I had an eating disorder. I agreed with everything he said and promised to cop myself on. Whole family watched me at dinner. Had second helpings. Mum cornered me later. Disaster. How can she possibly understand that I can't bear my gross body? I just want to be thin, that's all, I want my life to start. Went to bed after swearing that I was better now. Couldn't go to the bathroom as she was watching. Was desperate to get all that food out of my stomach. Puked into a plastic bag instead.

Points for discussion:

1. Behind every eating disorder is someone with low self-esteem. Why do you think so many young women have low self-esteem?
2. How can family and friends help someone with an eating disorder?
3. Eating disorders are on increase among young men. Why do you think this is?

Improvisations:

1. Elizabeth is hospitalised because of her eating disorder. It's visiting hour. Run the scene.
2. A supermodel dies from anorexia. Present a television news report, with interviews with her family, fashion designers, other models etc.

☆☆☆☆☆☆

HAIL MARY

LISA, AGED 17

Hail Mary full of Grace the Lord is with thee blessed art thou amongst women and all that. Mary, I feel a bit bad because I'm only here looking for another favour. I know I promised faithfully to visit you more often after the last one, but circumstances kind of conspired against me. And I know I shouldn't try to bargain with you, but if you answer my prayers today I'll come by every day for a whole month, I swear.

It's about this exam in the morning, Mary. Now, I'm not trying to say that it's more important to me than to anybody else. Sandra Pierce, a girl in my class, says she's going to commit suicide if she doesn't get an A or a B1 — she has an old skipping rope tied to her bedroom door for when the results come out, imagine that? She says that if she can't be a nuclear physicist, then she doesn't want to be anything at all.

So it's not as though this exam is more important to me than to Sandra Pierce. Although it is, in a way. I mean, what right has Sandra Pierce to go killing herself when her Da owns two Spars and three newsagents? Even if she gets a D3 tomorrow, it's not as though she'll ever be short of a job, is it?

Sorry Mary. I know it's a sin to be jealous. And I know that we all have our own cross to carry, it's just that sometimes it's hard to see what Sandra Pierce's is. But if she wants to be a nuclear physicist, then I hope she gets it.

As for myself, Mary, my ambitions wouldn't be that high. I'm only looking for a pass, or God willing, a C. I'd take Arts if I got it, or maybe a course in a regional college. I'd even consider a vocational qualification if it came to it. I'm not that fussy Mary, and I'm not that proud either.

But if I fail this exam tomorrow, Mary, I know where I'll end up. Not in a fancy newsagent's or a Dublin 4 Spar, but working part-time in my Da's filthy butchers and marrying some eejit just like my sister. I'll have a corporation flat and two kids by twenty and that'll be that, won't it? The end of my so-called life.

Points for discussion:

1. Is exam pressure too extreme?

2. Who puts on the pressure?

3. What other ways could schools or the Department of Education measure learning?

Improvisations:

1. Lisa gets teased by her friends for being a swot — she won't go to the disco on Friday because she's studying. Run the scene.

2. Improvise a group sitting a really tough exam — mostly mime as exams are silent! Lots of looking around and pencil tapping - try to build up a tension.

3. On the way to an important exam Tom/Tanya takes a detour to a park. He/She sits on a bench and considers not turning up at the exam. Run this scene using two people — one to play the character silently and the other to narrate what's going on in his/her head.

✿✿✿✿✿✿

FEAR AND LOATHING

SARAH JANE, AGE 17

I stand and wait in silence. My heart's pounding like a jackhammer and my knees are weak. With a huge effort, I bring my head up high and force a sneer to my lips. Invincible. That's me. A general about to lead the army into battle.

A snigger behind me, Joanne Murphy nudging Lisa Finn. I turn around and give her the thousand yard stare. Shut up I say and she does.

At last. A loud flush and a rustle. The door of the toilet swings open and there she stands, like some dumb rabbit rooted to the middle of the road just begging to be run over. She meets my eyes and you can almost hear her stomach churn in fright. She tries to sidle past towards the door but I reach out and grab her hard. Material rips and her skirt comes away in my hand. Joanne convulses in nervous laughter. Lisa brays. The rabbit shivers violently, bared to her expensive pink underwear. She spins around and tries to go back into the jacks but I jam my foot against the door. Wood splinters. Trapped.

Lisa and Joanne close in behind me, menace in the air. Not a sound now. All eyes bore into her. She presses hard against the wall, shrinks down, tries to disappear into her own skin. My heart beats faster.

Hello, I say softly. What what what do you want, she asks, stammering like an idiot. Extreme fright can do that, I've discovered. Don't know, I say. And I don't. A big house like hers? A posh address? A mother who makes my lunch in the morning instead of snoring her hangover off? A father who doesn't lift his hand by way of greeting? Her life, that's what I want, maybe. I don't know.

Money I say aloud, just to fill the silence. Don't don't don't have any, she squeaks. Twenty quid, I say nicely, as though she hasn't even spoken. She puts her hand out as though to touch me. I back off, afraid. TWENTY QUID TOMORROW I scream. She jumps in shock. Lisa and Joanne do too. I don't think I've ever felt this good.

You can go now, I say, and I love the indecision on her face. Either she walks out into the busy corridor in her knickers or she stays here with us. There's no contest really. She goes. She's gone.

I feel drained now, sick with myself and bone tired – so tired I could lie down and sleep on the hard tile floor. Just drift off and never wake up. But Joanne and Lisa are looking at me now, confused, troops without a leader. With a supreme effort, I throw back my shoulders and march out.

☆☆☆☆☆☆

Points for discussion:

1. Would this situation have been different if the other girls were not there? Are they responsible for what happened?

2. Could the victim of this have acted any differently?

3. What makes people bully others?

4. How could schools ensure that bullying doesn't happen?

Improvisations:

1. Gather all the people involved in the incident into the principal's office . . . What happens?

2. Two people sit beside each other on a bus and slowly one begins to intimidate the other, very subtly at first then leading to a confrontation or one person walking away.

    You can decide beforehand who will bully who, or not!

3. Walk around the room in these various manners: Aggressive, Confident, Slightly Nervous, Very Afraid.

    Then do a mix, letting people choose their own and interact with each other.

✸ ✸ ✸ ✸ ✸ ✸

BOYS'
Monologues

ER, UM, SEX

MICHAEL, AGED 13

It was pretty mortifying all around. He'd obviously been working himself up to it for weeks, and had even gone out and bought books and tapes and everything. One night he says in this kind of strangled squeak that it's time we had a chat about a few things. I was dying to see the end of Gladiators, but I could tell by the look on his face that he'd never get up the bottle again.

It was hilarious really, him trying to explain all about the birds and the bees — he even used that phrase — and how girls are essentially different to boys, as if that was some kind of revelation. Finally, he ran out of steam and turned in desperation to the books. One of them was about this geeky pair called Brian and Barbara and how their bodies changed as they were growing up. Me and Dad were treated to shots of Brian and Barbara's naked bodies in glorious Technicolor, with a few squeamish drawings of Barbara's innards and Brian's dangly bits. The book went very quiet on what Brian and Barbara get up to when they're not being photographed.

Poor Dad was shaking at this point, his forehead covered in sweat. I'd only ever seen him like that after that car accident involving Mr. Ryan.

Finally, the lesson ground to a halt and he asked me if I had any questions. I was going to ask him to run through it one more time just for the hell of it, but I thought he'd had enough for one night. It's all crystal clear Dad, I said.

You never saw anybody move so fast. Books were gathered up and the telly was on in a wink and he was sprinting for the door. He stopped to ask if I'd like to keep the books in case I found any of it confusing. I couldn't deceive him any longer. I said that I'd known all about that stuff for ages, learned it from mates and the TV. He looked annoyed then, as though I'd pulled one over on him. But then he sort of admitted that he'd known long before his Da had sat him down too. The next day, he traded in the books for a stack of golf manuals instead.

Points for discussion:

1. What is the best way for young people to learn about relationships and sexuality? From parents, teachers, friends, magazines?

2. Why do people get embarrassed discussing sexual matters?

Improvisations:

1. Michael's dad retreats to the pub for a pint with his friends. He tells them the ordeal he's just been through. Run the scene.

2. Two people have a conversation: For one the taboo topic is Transport of any kind, for the other it's Clothing of any kind. Try and steer the conversation away from the topic which makes you nervous and embarrassed.

3. Taboos:
   Try and describe
   - last night's soccer match without using these words: Ball, Score, Goal, or Pass.
   - your favourite band without saying: CD, Album, Lyrics, Music or their name!
   - how to make a cake without: Flour, Mix, Stir, Ingredients, or Oven!
   - how to get to your house without saying: Right, Road, or Street!

STICKS AND STONES

VINNIE, AGE 14

It's easy. You just clip out the letters you need from newspaper headlines, glue them onto a piece of paper, wrap the piece of paper securely around a fair-sized rock, hurl the rock through the window and Bob's your uncle. You get your message home, so to speak.

This one here, this says "Pushers Out", see? Fairly straight-forward, yeh? But the trouble is that the bloke who's gonna get this is fairly slow. We've broken nearly every one of the windows in his gaff at this stage and he hasn't got the message yet. He's still living in our estate and hanging around the corner shop like some kind of walking skeleton. But tonight we've a big campaign organised, he's gonna get no peace tonight. We'll drive him out sooner or later.

His Ma came to the door last week and shouted us down. He's a user alright, she screamed, but he's not a pusher. And she begged us to leave them alone. Some of the crowd cleared off then, but not me. No way. I've never seen him push myself, but nearly all of those junkies do. How else are they gonna get money for their rotten skag? Pusher or not, we have to live here and that gives us a right to say what kind of people we want as neighbours, doesn't it? And what kind we don't.

The cops will probably turn up tonight and arrest one or two of us for throwing stones. There's no evidence he's a pusher, they said at the last community meeting. If they want evidence they should look at the track marks on some of the kids around here.

It makes me laugh, I'll tell you. And it makes me get out there and do something about it, while the lefties are whinging about civil rights and the guards are fumbling about for evidence. Wait until it's one of their kids. Be a different story then.

I might make up another message just in case. Like I said, we've a big campaign organised tonight, I don't want to be caught short. He'll get no rest tonight.

Points for discussion:

1. Why do you think Vinnie is acting this way?
2. What are the dangers of vigilante action?

Improvisations:

1. Vinnie is arrested and brought to the local garda station. His parents are called to collect him. Run the scene.

2. A vigilante group are protesting outside a house. The person on their placards emigrated two weeks previously. Be the family inside — frightened and trying to tell them to leave.

✻ ✻ ✻ ✻ ✻ ✻

EVERYBODY ELSE IS DOING IT . . .

JASON, AGE 14

They were waiting for me when I got in. I knew straight away that something big was up. Where were you, says Da. Out, says I. Where, says Ma. With my mates, says I. Dad half-stands now but Ma pulls him back down. Where exactly did you go with your mates, you pup, says he. Feel blood draining from my face. Went for a walk, says I, knowing it sounded stupid. None of my mates will walk further than the fridge and my Da knows it. I try to look innocent but it doesn't wash. A sneer curls his lip. I know exactly where you were, says he. You were down in Finnegans. Ma looks like she's going to cry. I was not! I says, my knees like jelly. I went over to Christy's gaff and we just watched the telly, I gabble — after we went for a walk, of course. Da looks at me sadly now. A liar as well, he says. I feel terrible, I want to sink through the floor. Jack from next door saw you and your mates propping up the bar in Finnegans, he says. I open my mouth to deny the whole thing. A loud hiccup comes out instead. The game is up.

Sit down says Da eventually. I do. Silence for an eternity, with the pair of them looking at me like

I'd just ruined their lives. You've really disappointed us, says Ma quietly, and suddenly I feel like crying. Sorry, I manage, looking at the table. Da just shakes his head. You're not sorry, says he. You'll go out and do it again next Saturday night, won't you? I try to reason with him. Everybody does it, says I, all my mates, everyone I know. It's just a few drinks at the weekend, there's no harm in it. No harm? Da explodes. Drinking at your age, screwing up your liver and what little there is of your brain? I get thick now too. I'm not an alcoholic, I say, it's just a social thing. In my day, starts Da. I grit my teeth as he goes on about respect for yourself and decency and how he and his mates used to be happy to sit on the river bank with a couple of fishing rods on a Saturday night. Eventually I can stand no more. Things have changed since your day, Da, I say, things have moved on.

Well you've moved on about as far as you're going to go, says he — because you're staying in on Saturday nights from now on. I look at him in disbelief. You can't do that, says I, it's stupid, you can't go around treating me like a child. Feel sick now as I imagine the laugh my mates will have over this. He's grounded, Christy will go on, he's gonna join the young pioneers. You can't do that, I tell Da again.

We can because we trusted you, says Ma and you let us down. I look at the table. She stands to go to bed. We're not doing this for the fun of it, says she. Whatever you think, we're only looking out for you. They go to bed and leave me there, feeling sorry and angry at the same time. Stomach's starting to churn now, queasiness setting in. Shouldn't have had that last pint, didn't even want it but it was my round. I barely make it to the bathroom before I'm sick.

Points for discussion:

1. Why, do you think, do some teenagers drink alcohol?

2. What situations can arise when teenagers drink alcohol to excess?

Improvisations:

1. A bunch of teenagers are drinking cider in the corner of a local football pitch. One falls over in the dark, hits his/her head, and is knocked out. What happens?

2. Aine/Ian wakes up. She/He was drinking at a party the night before. She/He had no idea where she/he is. She/He's genuinely frightened. Run the scene as she/he tries to discover what has happened.

WINNER TAKES ALL

FINTAN, AGE 14

Two all. I check my watch. Only five minutes to the whistle and the crowd is going wild. It's not looking good. The wind's in our faces and the ref's on their side — ah come on, ref! That was a foul! Foul! Give that man a pair of glasses.

For the first time in living memory, we've reached the finals of the Inter–schools cup. Their team is faster, slicker and their shiny green gear is sponsored by the local supermarket. Our Dotsy is out there in borrowed shorts and his brothers' boots. Oh, they're confident alright. And they're hungry for it. But after ten years at the bottom of the league, we're more than hungry. We're desperate.

Dotsy with the ball now, up the left wing, watch your back! Wiry strength as he dodges a six footer in green, looks around to pass. As usual, there's not a friendly face in sight. Ah lads, will you give him a hand out there! Too late. Six green jerseys jump on Dotsy; the ref turns a blind eye.

Everyone on this side of terrace jumps to their feet and the chant begins. Dot-sy! Dot-sy! Never seen such a turn-out before, it's brilliant. Imelda Maguire and her gang screaming their guts out right alongside arch-enemies Barry and Dave. Dot-sy!

Since we got through the first round last October, it's like everyone's gone mad. First time our school won anything except a bad reputation. We'll show them yet. We'll show them.

Two minutes to go and you could cut the air with a knife. Oh no. A green jersey has the ball and he's belting down the pitch, poor Jeremy in goal is wetting his pants. It looks like it's all over as our defenders fall one by one, the domino effect. The green jersey is inside the twenty five yard line now, Jeremy is frozen with fright. I shut my eyes as the roar goes up. I feel sick.

But it's our side roaring. Jeremy's clutching the ball to his chest and grinning like a fool. Kick it out! we scream, you can grin later. For the first time in his life, Jeremy delivers a perfect shot, high in the air and up the pitch. The ball lands right at Dotsy's feet. He spins around and goes with it.

Dot-sy! Dot-sy! Up the field he flies, weaving, dodging, out-running one green jersey, then two more. The shouts die down as we watch, open-mouthed, as Dotsy is transformed into Pele for a day. He seems to float above the ground as he makes for the goal, his face twisted into a desperate grimace of pain. The opposition are left standing as he sails past, the ball welded to his foot. His flight is suspended for only a moment as he aims a kick at the ball. It sails through the air as if in slow motion. Their goalie lunges left and high. He misses. The ball hits the back of the net a second before the whistle blows.

Insanity erupts on the terrace. Lunacy, madness and elation. We've won. We've won.

✻ ✻ ✻ ✻ ✻ ✻

Points for discussion:

1. Why do people like sports?

2. Do you think P.E. is as important (or more important!) as the other subjects in school?

3. Do you think sport should be compulsory in schools or should people make their own choice?

Improvisations:

1. Be a crowd at a match cheering on your team.

2. Be a sports commentator live on air commentating on your favourite sport.

3. Mime: Form a circle with one person in the middle who will mime a sport. Others join in when they recognise it. When everybody has joined in stop and start again.

✻✻✻✻✻✻

HARMLESS PICTURES?

IAN, AGED 15

I'm in for it now. No getting out of this one. She's already given off steam but she's not finished yet by a long shot, oh no. She's over there now making a big statement by tearing it up and stuffing it into the bin page by page. She says that she's finished with me, but I know she doesn't mean it. She couldn't be serious about finishing with me over a stupid magazine. Could she?

Wasn't even any of her business. Snooping, as usual. She says that her pen fell on the floor and she saw the magazine lying there under my bed, plain as day. Why would I bother hiding it, I said to her, it's not as though every bloke in the world doesn't get his hands on one at some stage. I mean, come on, they do. That got her even more riled. She said that I was wrong, that not every guy gets a kick out of looking at naked women, women who were . . . what was it? Oh yeh, "contorted into degrading positions". That made me angry then, the way she was implying that I was a pervert or something. It's only stupid, harmless pictures, I said to her, it's not like I think that's what women are really like. And she said that she personally felt cheapened because of that magazine, imagine that! By my choice of reading matter, I have somehow made her cheap! I told her that she was getting on her feminist high-horse then, and she said that it wasn't particularly feminist to worry about getting raped by some creep who's filled up on skin magazines and videos. That really made me sick. Now I'm a rapist, a woman-hater who should be locked up and the key thrown away. I told her that she was two-faced, that most people get turned on by some of that stuff or at least they're curious. And that she was just being sanctimonious for the sake of it. She gave me one of those looks then, the looks girls give to guys to remind us that they're the superior sex. And she announced that she was finished with me.

She's still over there, tearing up that magazine and thinking up new arguments to throw at me. Oh, I'm in for it yet, there's no getting out of this one. Finished with me, my eye. She's only getting started.

Points for discussion:

1. What is pornography?
2. Who should decide what is to be censored?

Improvisations:

1. Organise a picket outside a video shop which rents pornographic videos. Argue with customers going in and out. Argue with the owner etc.

2. Run a Radio Talk Show item about a well-known pop group's new single being banned from the airwaves. Take calls from all sides.

3. Mime: There is a billboard at your local train station that offends some people.

   It's morning rush hour and as people arrive for their train they react to it.

✻ ✻ ✻ ✻ ✻ ✻

LOOSE TALK

PAUL, AGE 15

I'm going to walk right up that path and knock on that door and ask to speak to her. I am. In two seconds, I'm going to knock on that door. Two seconds. I just need to get my head together first, that's all. I just need a moment to sort myself out. Okay. Do it now. Do it.

Maybe this isn't such a good idea. I mean, what if she doesn't want to see me? Worse still, what if she's told her Da the whole story and *he* wants to see me? Although I wouldn't blame her. Wouldn't blame her at all.

It might be better if I wrote her a letter. You know, get it all down on paper, clear and precise, tell her exactly how bad I feel about the whole thing. Yeh.

But she'd probably say that was cowardly, even more cowardly than what I've already done. She's very straight, is Jodie. Very straight and honest and down the line. It'd be easier if she wasn't, in a way.

There's a light gone on in her bedroom window now. I was in there once — in her bedroom. It was perfectly innocent, she was just lending me some tapes. We were only ever friends, me and her. Not anymore.

I don't know what possessed me to tell that lie. Was sick of the slagging and the jokes, I suppose, sick of being the only one who's never had a girlfriend. I know it's no excuse, but I just said it off the top of my head, didn't stop to think, just blurted out that me and Jodie had done it. And then it was too late, they wanted all the gory details and the lie just grew bigger and bigger until I was making up a blow-by-blow account of what had supposedly happened in that bedroom. I felt awful at the time, but I consoled myself with the thought that at least it wouldn't get back to her.

It did. She never said a word. She just gave me a look that made me feel so small and so stupid. I wished she'd screamed and shouted, called me all the names under the sun. But she never said a word — not then and not when I came clean with my mates and admitted that I'd made the whole thing up.

In two seconds I'm gonna go up to that door and ring the bell and ask to speak to her and I'm gonna apologise. It's not like I expect everything to be the same as before — I know it's too late for that — but I want her to know that I'm sorry. I'm gonna go now. In two seconds. I just need to get my head together first.

✹ ✹ ✹ ✹ ✹ ✹

Points for discussion:

1. Why do you think Paul lied?

2. Do you think that young people are often influenced by peer group pressure? Do you think adults are influenced also?

Improvisations:

1. Paul knocks on the door and Jodie answers. Run the scene.

2. Run the scene where Paul tells his friends that he lied.

✺ ✺ ✺ ✺ ✺ ✺

READY OR NOT

STEVEN, AGE 16

Sarah? Sarah, are you alright in there? Well what's taking you so long then? Sarah? Sarah, now I'm not trying to rush you or anything, but the parents are due home in about half an hour, so we'd want to hurry up if we're going to . . . you know . . .

Sarah, you're not worried, are you? Because you shouldn't be. Nothing will go wrong, I've taken care of that side of things, you know I'd never let anything go wrong in that department. Alright? Good, good. Sarah, is that the shower going again? You've already had one . . . Ah Sarah, you're not all nervous about it, are you? Well so am I, if it makes you feel any better. And it's not like we haven't talked it through, eh? It's not like we haven't discussed every single aspect of this, and planned for it, it's not as though it's a spur of the moment kind of thing. We love each other, and it's a perfectly natural part of loving someone, right? You said so yourself. But the time has come, Sarah, for the talking to stop and for there to be some action . . . I mean . . . some . . . you know what I mean.

Sarah? Are you listening to me? Sarah! Ah come on Sarah, you're not going to mess me about again this time, are you? How many times have you done this, eh? Gone so far, got my hopes up and then you change your mind, just like that? Yeh I am getting annoyed, and would you blame me? You go on and on about me putting pressure on you but if you have no intention of ever doing it, then why don't you give us both a break and just say it? Be straight with me? I'll be straight and say that yeh I want to, that yeh I'd like it to be with you, but I'm not going to save myself until I'm married, I'm only young, right? And no Sarah, that wasn't a threat to finish with you if you won't put out, that's an awful thing to say, you think that we're all a bunch of creeps only after one thing . . .

[loud noise]

Was that you? Sarah, I'm serious. Was that you making that noise? No? Oh God. The parents are home.

Points for discussion:

1. Why is Sarah not coming out?

2. Is Steven being too impatient?

Improvisations:

1. Enter parents. Run the scene!

2. Sarah decides to chat to her mum, what happens?

3. Sarah's mum rings Steven's mum and is very anxious!

4. Swap genders on the monologue — Steven locks himself in and Sarah tries some persuading!

✷ ✷ ✷ ✷ ✷ ✷

JECKYL AND HYDE, HIDE

NICK, AGE 16

We all huddle in my bed, the three of us, frozen in the dark. Tommy starts to cry. Shut up, I hiss, do you want to bring him up here? He shakes his head mutely and is quiet. Now Orla wants to go to the toilet. Well you can't, I tell her. Not yet.

We were all woken an hour ago by the racket downstairs. He'd said he was just popping out to get the evening paper. Two hours later he still wasn't back. Ma packed us off to bed, her face tight and red, and told us not to stir until the morning. She knew what was coming. We all did. Sometimes I hate him so much I want to kill him.

I'm going to burst, Orla whispers now, shifting on the bed. Burst then, I whisper back. Because if you go out there he'll hear you and you don't want that, do you? She doesn't. She bites her lip and clamps her knees together tight. I put my arm around her. He'll pass out soon, I tell her, and it'll be alright.

Raised voices downstairs now, him trying to pick a fight. Ma pleading with him, trying to calm him down. The more she pleads the angrier he gets, that's the way it always goes. Then maybe he'll belt her one, depending on how drunk he is. When I'd see the bruises in the mornings I'd ask why she bothered talking to him, why she didn't just leave him down there in the kitchen on his own. She didn't answer, just looked at Tommy and Orla and I knew that if he couldn't hit her, then he'd probably hit us.

I want to go down there now, to face up to him, drunk bully that he is. I'm nearly as big and tall as him now and I'd love to smash his face in to give him a taste of his own medicine. How can he be a normal, nice father for most of the week and then on Friday night he'll get drunk and turn into a monster that none of us knows?

He'll be sorry in the morning, he always is. He'll sit at breakfast pretending that everything is fine. He'll be all over Tommy and Orla, doing stupid tricks with the cutlery to make them laugh. He jokes with me as though nothing at all had happened the night before, and it's funny, but you start to believe it yourself. And you believe it all week until the weekend comes around again and he'll say that he's just going out for the paper, or to borrow something from a mate. Two hours later, we're all silent and afraid, happy families down the drain.

A shout from downstairs and then a loud crash. We all tense. But then Mum's voice, normal and low. She's alright, he's just fallen over again. The stairs creaking now, as he lumbers up them, Mum close behind. Orla and Tommy huddle closer, baby faces frozen in fear. Footsteps unsteadily pass our door and then we hear springs creaking in the next room as he collapses onto the bed. Silence falls over the house again. It's okay, I tell Orla and Tommy. He's asleep.

❅ ❅ ❅ ❅ ❅ ❅

Points for discussion:

1. What effects do you think an alcoholic parent has on a family?

2. Is it particularly hard for Nick because he is the eldest?

Improvisations:

1. Nick's father is hospitalised for his alcoholism. He wants to make a fresh start. It's family visiting day. Run the scene.

2. The Gardai arrest Nick's father for violent behaviour. Nick goes to visit him. Run the scene.

❅ ❅ ❅ ❅ ❅ ❅

FOOTSTEPS

GARY, AGE 17

He's in there now watching the eating habits of the black-horned hump-backed almost-extinct blind mountain fowl and loving every minute of it. In an hour's time, he'll switch over to Farmer's Weekly in the hope that there might be some footage of a sheep shearing contest and if all else fails, he'll tune in to Animal Hospital. He's a vet, my Dad, and he never knows when to leave the job behind.

Never knows when to leave his illusions behind either. For my last birthday, he proudly presented me with my very own calving jack, which has more or less the same function as a forceps, only it's used for calf births as opposed to the human kind.

That night he got me out of bed at 4am, beside himself with excitement, and dragged me off to help with Rocky Smith's Fresian cow who was trying her best to calve. The Fresian hated me on sight, the calving jack broke in two and the calf slid out all by itself the minute my back was turned. My father and Rocky Smith laughed like it was some big joke and handed me a lump of straw to dry off my frozen, bloody hands. I'm no good at this, I tried to tell Da on the way back in the car, shivering and smelling of dung. You'll learn, he replied smugly and whistled cheerfully the rest of the way home.

Lately he's been moaning about his back and hinting that the practise is getting too big for him. He's been dragging me out on calls with him more and more. It's never been said, but it doesn't take a genius to see what he's doing. To him, the company of smelly, diseased animals, coupled with low pay, little gratitude and no holidays is a great life. To me, it's no life at all.

The problem is telling Dad. I mean really telling him, as opposed to dropping a few broad hints like I've been doing over the last year. The CAO form has to be handed in tomorrow and I've it all filled out except for my first course choice. It'll break his heart, Mum said earlier, in a very quiet voice. I don't want to break his heart, but I have to go my own way, don't I?

I'll just wait until the blind mountain fowl has done its thing. Then I might watch a bit of Farmer's Weekly with him and break it to him gently, the way I've learned from him over the years as he's told Rocky Smith or Jim Ryan or Anto Moran that their prize heifer has just died.

Points for discussion:

1. Should parents influence their children's career choices?

2. Why do you think it's important to his father that Gary follow in his footsteps?

Improvisations:

1. It's dinnertime and Gary's younger sister suddenly announces she wants to be a vet. What's the reaction?

2. A Christmas family gathering, Gary has just finished his first term in college in Dublin studying History of Art and French. Run the scene using cousins, uncles, aunts, neighbouring farmers etc . . . and of course Gary's parents!

3. Mime Game:
   What's my job — join in! Form a circle with one person in the middle. This person chooses a job and mimes it. As others think they recognise the job they step forward and join him/her in the workplace, miming also. Communication in this game must be by physical actions only — part of the fun is having others join you who are on the wrong track! When everyone is involved it is time to stop and start again.

✵ ✵ ✵ ✵ ✵ ✵

OH BABY PLEASE!

ANDREW, AGE 17

I am your spaniel, Demetrius, and the more you beat me I will fawn on you. Spurn me, strike me, neglect me, lose me . . . Ah Cassandra, will you ever stop that whinging, eh? Come on now, I'm trying to learn this for tomorrow and you're not helping. Shush, there's a good girl. Now I know you can't be hungry, I gave you a bottle only an hour ago, so stop. You're not sick, are you? Don't be sick on me, please, because I won't have a clue what to do. Listen, your Ma will be by to collect you later, can you hang on until then? Yeh? Ah Cassandra, please! Do you want to make me ring her and drag her away from her mates, and this the first night she's had out since you were born? And you know what she'll say, don't you? She'll say that your Da hasn't a clue and can't be trusted with you for one single night. And then *her* Ma will jump on the bandwagon and say that I'm a loser who got her daughter in trouble and that she should keep you well away from me. And that'll sicken me altogether. Come on Cassandra, stop crying, please!

Come here, do you want to hear a story, yeh? Once upon a time there was this bloke called Demetrius, and this girl Helena who was absolutely crazy about him, but didn't he love someone else called Hermia, right? She was better looking or something. But Helena hung in there, she says to him that even if he treated her like a dog, she'd still love him, isn't that a good one? No, I can see you're not all that impressed.

Maybe I should ring my Ma. Yeh, I'll ring my Ma down the bingo and she'll be able to tell me if there's something really wrong with you or if you're just acting the maggot. And you know what, Cassandra? I'll feel all embarrassed and inadequate because before you know it, she'll be home and doting on you and I'll be banished upstairs, out in the cold. And this is supposed to be our night Cassandra, yours and mine. And if you had any appreciation at all, you'd stop crying and let me get on with my homework or I'll never finish school and get a decent job and you'll have no kind of a life at all. So there.

Good girl. See? I knew you'd stop crying for me. Ssssh. God, you're gorgeous, do you know that? You're absolutely gorgeous when you smile. No, I'm perfectly serious, you're gonna be a stunner when you grow up.

Didn't I say from the very start that you took after your old man?

☆ ☆ ☆ ☆ ☆ ☆

Points for discussion:

1. Are men as good with babies as women?

2. What are the disadvantages of having a baby while still in school? What are the advantages?

Improvisations:

1. Cassandra is now ten months old and Andrew takes her in her buggy to the park.

   They're having lunch and managing fine — yet a few of middle-aged women can't resist making "helpful" remarks and suggestions! Run the scene.

2. Bring your two year old to your local shopping centre, where she/he meets other parents and toddlers. Half the class play adults, half play toddlers — then swap over.

3. Circle Game: One person is chosen and leaves the room. The others — all playing two-year-olds — form a circle and place an object in the centre (anything! — hair slide, piece of clothing, book, pencil etc.) The chosen person returns — everybody in the circle must sit still and cry and until the chosen person brings them "their" object. The only help they can offer is to point to their object ... or to complain bitterly if it is given to somebody else! When there is a beautiful silence, this game is finished.

   This game can give a sense of the tremendous pressure relentless crying can cause!

OUT OF CONTROL

TOMMY, AGE 17

I couldn't believe it when I'd done it, I just couldn't. One second she was standing right there in front of me and the next she was flat on her back. For a wild moment, I thought that she'd actually fainted. But when she looked up at me like she was terrified, I realised that I had hit her. I'd punched her right in the chest.

I don't know who was more shocked, me or her. I'd never laid a finger on her before, never. I mean, I think the world of her, I always have. We'd had our arguments like everybody else, but nothing like this. I felt so awful that I got down on my hands and knees and hugged her and apologised to her. I swore it would never happen again, ever. And I meant every word of it, I really did.

We had a long talk and I persuaded her to stay. I put the whole thing out of my mind, because that wasn't me, not the real me. Things went well for a while and then another argument erupted. It was over something stupid, but it was her way of talking down to me like I was really thick that got under my skin. It was like I lost control. I hit her.

Later, I tried to understand why I did it, tried to explain to her that when I got angry, I couldn't get the words out and so the reflexes took over instead. She said she didn't care and that she wasn't taking any more of it.

For a week, I phoned and sent flowers and passed messages through her friends. By some miracle, we started going out again, on the condition that I got some help. Professional help, she elaborated, to combat my problem. I agreed right away.

Between one thing and another, I never did. I mean, I would have if I thought I'd had a real problem, but it had only happened twice. Besides, I knew my weaknesses now and how to control them. Me and her were getting on better than ever at this stage, and those two nights were just like a bad dream.

Which is why I can't believe I did what I did last night. And all over what stupid club we'd go to, can you believe that? I hit her in the middle of the street. I was completely sick with myself, I tried to tell her how sorry I was but she just walked away. I was all set to go around to her place this morning to apologise, but I found myself giving a statement instead. She's pressing charges, the guards said, and we're not short of witnesses.

The older guard paused at the door. He said that he had two daughters about her age and it turned his stomach to think of them coming up against scum like me. I tried to explain, tried to tell him that the last thing I ever meant to do was hurt her, but he closed the door in my face.

Points for discussion:

1. Why do you think Tommy was violent?

2. What do you think should happen when it goes to court?

3. What are good ways to express anger?

Improvisations:

1. Tell the story from Tommy's girlfriend's perspective.

2. Interview Tommy for a television documentary on domestic violence. Interview his mother, father and girlfriend.

✿ ✿ ✿ ✿ ✿ ✿